The Hand of Apollo

ALSO BY ELIZABETH COATSWORTH

The Cave
Desert Dan
The Noble Doll
Jock's Island

The Hand of Apollo

Elizabeth Coatsworth

Illustrated by Robin Jacques

The Viking Press / New York

Library of Congress catalog card number: 65-18156
Fiction 1. Greece, ancient—Stories

Second printing January 1966

The poetry on pages 14 and 38 is from Homer, translated by Robert
Payne in his book *The Splendor of Greece*, copyright 1960, Harper and
Row, Publishers. Used by permission.

The poetry on pages 25, 26, and 50–51 is adapted from J. W. Mackail's
Select Epigrams from the Greek Anthology.

PRINTED IN THE U. S. A. BY VAIL-BALLOU PRESS

To Henry,
the classicist of the family,
with my love.

The Hand of Apollo

Chapter 1

About the middle of the fourth century before Christ those half-Greeks, Philip of Macedon and later his son, Alexander the Great, swept down from the north and subdued the Greek cities one by one. When Alexander was dead, and his conquests in Persia and the East divided among his generals, the Macedonian garrison remained in Corinth for more than a hundred years—a heavy weight on the city's pride and love of freedom. In the end it was the Romans whom Corinth had to thank for the removal of the Macedonians, and when the people heard the news they cheered so loudly that it is said that crows flying overhead dropped dead out of the sky.

But that freedom was as short-lived as the freedom of the frogs who exchanged King Log for King Stork. Soon the Romans began to assume increasing authority until at last in

146 B.C., fifty years after the Romans' first coming, the Achaean League, led by Corinth, raised a hopeless rebellion against them and was defeated on the isthmus in the last great Greek battle for freedom.

Now Lucius Mummius, Roman general and consul, sat by the shore of the Gulf of Corinth with the great gilded city behind him, rising terrace upon terrace to the many-colored temples on the heights of the Acrocorinth. Lucius Mummius preferred not to look at the scene. He had decided to make an example of Corinth and had given orders that the rich and noble city was to be leveled to the ground, its men put to the sword, and its women and children taken into slavery. But there was great wealth to be collected before the buildings were given to the flames, and Mummius now sat watching a long procession of soldiers passing by to the harbor, carrying the statues of gods and heroes taken from the temples and street corners. Each treasured object was checked by army secretaries before it was stowed away in the waiting galleys. At any clumsiness, the general winced.

"If you break that Apollo, you'll have to replace it with one as good!" he shouted to a man who had stumbled. "It's worth your hide, twenty times over!"

A respectful secretary approached.

"There is a man here who claims Roman citizenship," he began.

But Mummius interrupted, "Later! Later! He can wait! Bring that little nymph nearer so I can see her," he called to another group of soldiers carrying a smaller statue than the Apollo.

"It came from the grotto," a centurion said, saluting.

"Put it in the vessel taking my things," Mummius ordered. "I like that blue flowered robe and her downcast look."

Instantly in his mind's eye he saw the new statue by the pool at his own villa in Italy—but would he ever look at it without a pang? Beauty is born like a flower and dies like a flower, but it was by his human decision and through his orders that the beauty of Corinth would soon lie withered among the stones.

Now prisoners were being led past him, mostly young women and children with a scattering of older men, craftsmen in marble and gold and in the fine pottery for which the city was famous. They would be useful when put to work in Rome. Now, herded like sheep toward the galleys, they went past Mummius, walking proudly. Would they still be walking so proudly when he saw them in Rome, his own slaves or the slaves of friends? Pride! Pride! Corinth had always been proud. Yesterday Mummius had seen how well her men fought, more bravely indeed than any of the other Greek allies, which was his excuse for the revenge he was taking. Once there had been philosophers in Corinth, but today people called it a city of traders. What learning is left among them, he wondered, these people of whom he had chosen— almost on a whim—to make slaves?

"You!" he called to a passing Corinthian boy. "Come here! I wish to speak to you."

The boy neither turned his head nor slackened his pace, but the Roman soldier beside him seized his shoulder and spun him around to face the general.

Mummius looked into gray eyes which stared back at him without expression.

"Write something, boy, there in the sand," he commanded.

"What?" asked the boy.

"Anything that comes into your head."

Without a further glance, the boy leaned down and, smoothing the damp sand, wrote swiftly two lines from Homer:

> Thrice and four times blessed
> are those who fell
> On the plain of Troy, obeying
> the will of the gods.

Yes, thought Lucius Mummius, in the fighting I was a soldier doing my duty as a soldier. I feel no sorrow for the Greeks left lying on the field of battle. There were plenty of dead Romans beside them to keep them company. But the murder of a great city—shall I ever cleanse my hands of this day's doing? At least I can make a gesture to placate the gods of Corinth.

"Go," he said to the boy. "You are free."

The boy straightened. "Where shall I go?" he asked.

"How do I know?" exclaimed the Roman. "It's your country." Then to one of the secretaries he said, "Give him a safe conduct."

Already he half regretted the impulse which had made him exempt this one prisoner from the universal death or slavery. He had wanted to make an atonement, but the boy's eyes had not lightened, or had he uttered one word of thanks.

I should behave just so in his place, Mummius thought, but it was as if an omen had gone wrong. The gods of Corinth were angry. He shrugged the thought from him.

"Where is the fellow who claims to be a Roman?" he demanded, turning away.

A middle-aged man stepped forward. "I am he," he said. "Sabinus, son of Lucinius of Frezellae, a Roman citizen who, by the order of the senate, settled in Delos."

"I know the family," said Mummius. "Greetings, Sabinus. Your father and now you have worked well in fostering friendship between Greeks and Romans."

For one moment the eyes of Sabinus swept along the line of loot and prisoners. "Yes. We have used many fair words and they were believed, for we, too, believed them."

"Enough of that!" said Mummius. "Your mother was Greek, I think? Your speech does not smack of Rome. Well, what is your claim, claiming to be a Roman?"

"I claim, as a Roman, the right to take my vessel back to Delos."

"What brought you here? Supplies for our enemies?"

"No. I did not know the armies were here. We have been trading along the coast. Some of the wine we carried was for Corinth."

"By rights I should order your ship seized with the other Greek vessels to help transport all this back to Rome. But Sabinus, I as a Roman send you, a Roman, on your way in safety. Remember that when you remember this day."

The secretary, who had been listening, wrote out a second pass, this time for the *Sea-Swallow* bound for Delos. Sabinus thanked the general curtly and turned on his heel.

"A fair wind," Mummius called after him in a tone half friendly, half contemptuous.

"My thanks, Lucius Mummius," the trader repeated over his shoulder. It was not a day when Rome or Romans pleased him.

Some hours later Sabinus was making his way along the beach toward his vessel. He carried his cloak over one arm, arranged so that no casual glance would see that it was looped into a sack hidden by the cloak's ornamental border. For once I have been "rich enough to go to Corinth," he thought, and then he was not pleased to have made a joke of the old proverb. He was both angry and distressed by the fate of Corinth, but, after all, he was a trader, and no trader could stand by and see such riches flow past him without dipping in his own hand for a share. The goblets of finest clay signed by the artists who had painted them, the ivory rouge box from Egypt, the length of cloth dyed purple-red with Tyrian mollusks, each was selected for its lightness and value after a careful assessment of the Roman who had possessed himself of it. Wine had been part of the payment, and if money had passed, no one had seen it slip from hand to hand.

The stupid fools! thought Sabinus. When did a Roman know beauty when he saw it?

He was glad the business was over. Looting and smuggling were dangerous for outsiders in time of war, but the centurions couldn't be everywhere. Nevertheless, he gave Lucius Mummius's chair a wide berth. The general, or one of his staff, still sat on in the dusk superintending the loading of people and treasure. Carefully as his cloak was arranged, Sabinus wanted no measuring glance to fall upon it.

Walking southward toward the Saronic Gulf, he almost

stepped on a boy who lay face downward in a hollow of the sand, his head in his arms, unmoving.

For a moment Sabinus stood looking down. Then he seated himself, his gaze fixed upon the water as though contemplating the scene before him, which included his own vessel anchored not far off.

"Are you the boy to whom Lucius Mummius gave safe conduct?" he asked in a low voice.

"Yes," said the boy. He had not been asleep, it seemed.

"What is your name?"

"Dion."

"Son of whom?"

"Dion, son of Hermonax."

"But Hermonax is—was—one of the Corinthian leaders!" Sabinus exclaimed, startled.

The boy said nothing.

"Are you not descended from the great Timoleon who put down the tyrant of Syracuse?"

"Yes."

"It is lucky that Mummius knew nothing of this, or you'd be in chains, ready to follow his chariot when they vote him a Roman triumph. But Mummius has a restless mind. Your quotation caught his fancy. He will ask about you."

The boy said nothing.

"Where are you going?"

"I do not know. Tonight I will go somewhere."

"Your father?"

"Dead."

"Your mother?"

"When the news came of our defeat, she took my little sister in her arms. One moment they were on the well curb and then they were—gone."

"And you?"

"After that I went out into the street with my tutor. They killed him while they held me back. One man wanted to kill me too, but the others said no, I was young enough to be put among the slaves. I wanted to die, but I had my father's orders."

"To live?"

"Yes. It would be much easier to die."

Sabinus was silent for a little.

"You and I have safe conducts, so we should stick together. Here on land you'd never get out of Roman reach. But there's a chance of it by sea."

"It might cost you your vessel."

"Yes. One must take a risk once in a while."

The boy raised his head and in the dusk stared at Sabinus.

"Why are you doing this?"

"Because I am half Greek and tonight my Greek half has the Roman by the throat. Like Lucius Mummius, I should like to expiate some of the guilt of Corinth by a small act."

"He felt guilt?"

"Oh, yes, guilty before the gods and citizens of Corinth, before great Corinth herself. I can smell guilt, having felt it most of my life."

In the early dusk, the boy's gray eyes were intent.

"Most of your life? Not just now for being a Roman citizen?"

"All my youth I was a Greek to my father and a Roman to my mother, never the thing each had hoped for."

Dion gave a long sigh.

"So it is with me. My father was always disappointed in me. Against his will, I dedicated myself to poetry and to Apollo of the Lyre."

"But Apollo is one of the most glorious of the gods, why did your father object?"

"My father wished me to follow in the footsteps of our family and to become a leader of the people in peace and war, not a poet, however renowned. I obeyed him in all things, but unwillingly. My heart was elsewhere."

Again the older man was silent.

When he spoke he said only, "Time heals. My parents grew to accept me as they had made me. Later your father would have been proud of you. Who knows? Perhaps we follow the god who chooses us and have ourselves no choice in the matter."

Dion sat up.

"Apollo chose, you think? Not I?"

"So I think. Only the gods know."

"If it were true, it would be a great weight off my heart."

"I think it is true."

For a little while the two sat together looking out over the darkening gulf.

Then Sabinus spoke briskly.

"The vessel below us is the *Sea-Swallow,* my ship. I shall go aboard now. By the time Cassiopeia is high in heaven the crew will be asleep in their quarters. Only the night watch will be awake, he and I. I shall leave a rope over the side and when I see you, I will engage the watch in talk at the bow. Come aboard. Untie the rope, coil it and take it with you to my tent at the stern. Go on your hands and knees so that you do not show above the rail. There is a rolled sheepskin at the back of the tent on which you may sleep. I shall come soon with bread and cheese for you."

"Your crew is Greek, but they would betray me if they knew?"

"Who can measure a man's heart? Some will betray for money and some out of fear."

Chapter 2

For eleven days and nights Dion lived in a shadowed world. All day the sun and the flocking darkness of clouds crossed the striped canvas of the small pavilion on the afterdeck which was the captain's quarters. When the flap at the front of the tent was thrown back, the boy stayed, standing or sitting, hidden by Sabinus's great cloak, hung from a support. Only the cabin boy Nico came near the place, once a day early, to straighten Sabinus's pallet and put his clothes in order.

"But you leave me no work, Master," he told Sabinus, with laughter in his voice. "You have grown so neat these days, and you eat more than you have ever eaten before. This voyage has brought you health."

"It is always so, Nico, when the *Sea-Swallow* sails for home," the captain said. "So soon now we should be seeing Mount Cynthus rising above the harbor. It will be good to be on Delos once more."

Dion, hidden behind the cloak, listened. Now instead of eyes, he depended on his ears, and there had been a note of amusement in Nico's voice, which lay deeper than his words. What had the ship's boy seen? What had he guessed? What would he do? Wait and see, wait and see, said the waves against the hull of the *Sea-Swallow*. Wait, wait, creaked the ropes, as the sailors, to the cries of the boatswain, hoisted or lowered the bright sails. See! See! See! shrieked the gulls overhead. The Fates will show, the Fates will show, the Fates will show, groaned and hissed the breakers along the rocks as they coasted the headlands.

The worst has already happened, thought Dion. What happens now will happen to me, and that doesn't matter.

But suppose it happened to Sabinus, too, for having given him shelter? Such thoughts could still trouble Dion, even in the midst of the unhappy memories which haunted him day and night. By day he kept them at bay by endlessly reciting long passages from Homer, Sophocles, Euripides, anything that he had ever learned by heart, and which he could now soundlessly chant as a charm to hold back his own terrible thoughts. But at night he had no protection against them. In his dreams all the horrors he had seen repeated themselves, sometimes in strange disguises, and sometimes interspersed by fragments of happy dreams in which he walked with his father and mother toward one of the temples, while his little sister ran ahead, gathering flowers. Then the nightmares would come again, the worse for the short release, and he would wake up groaning, Sabinus's hand shaking his shoulder and his whisper in his ear.

Meantime, the voyage itself went smoothly and each evening Sabinus dropped a white pebble into a jar to mark a good day's voyage.

But toward sundown one day, as they neared the Piraeus, a small, fast vessel overhauled and passed them and disappeared into the dusk. "A Roman courier," said Sabinus. "She travels late, bringing trouble for someone," but, unsuspecting for whom the trouble was intended, he once again added a white pebble to those already in the jar, leaving the ill-omened black pebbles untouched in their place.

Dion had never been on shipboard before. Even preoccupied by grief as he was, he could not help being aware of the motion of the *Sea-Swallow,* of her dartings and checkings, of her rollings and curvettings, of the wind in the rigging and the smell of salt, pitch, and spilled wine. He learned to distinguish the voices of the unseen crew and came to know their sailors' songs, and at night, as he lay on the sheepskin, he lifted the hangings a little to see the stars which seemed to sway in the dark heavens with every movement of the vessel.

In bad weather Sabinus ate the meals Nico brought him, in his chair by the open door of the tent, under cover. When it was fair he ate beneath the open sky.

"Ah, Nico," he said one day, "this is such a moment as the poet Antiphilus meant when he wrote 'Mine be a mattress on the poop, and the awnings over it sounding with the blows of the spray, and the fire forcing its way out of the hearthstones, and a pot upon them with the empty turmoil of bubbles; and let me see the boy dressing the meat, and may my table be a ship's plank covered with a fresh cloth.' "

"When did you take to reciting poetry, Master? You have changed, indeed."

"Numskull! Do I not come from Delos where the great Apollo himself was born? And you! If you honored the god, you would listen with more attention."

"If you must recite," said Nico, "I could wish you better ears than mine. Who knows? A spirit may overhear you." There was again that hidden laughter in the boy's voice of which Dion was so aware, but Sabinus seemed to find nothing amiss.

"So far all has gone well and I have dropped no black pebble in the jar," Sabinus said. "This afternoon I shall offer a libation to Poseidon and the Nereids." Again leaning back in his chair, which creaked a little under the change of weight, he recited: " 'Now is the season for the ship to run through the gurgling water, and no longer does the sea gloom, fretted with gusty squalls, and now the swallow plasters her round house under the rafters, and the soft leafage laughs in the meadows. Therefore wind up your soaked cables, O sailors, and stretch the forestays to carry your well-woven sails. This I bid you, I, the god of the anchorage.' "

"Have you finished, sir?"

"With food or with poetry? With both, Nico, with both! Take yourself and the dishes off. You are all alike empty!"

But Sabinus seemed in good humor and Dion was sure that the recitation had been intended for him, not for Nico. This was a side of Sabinus he had not guessed. For a moment he

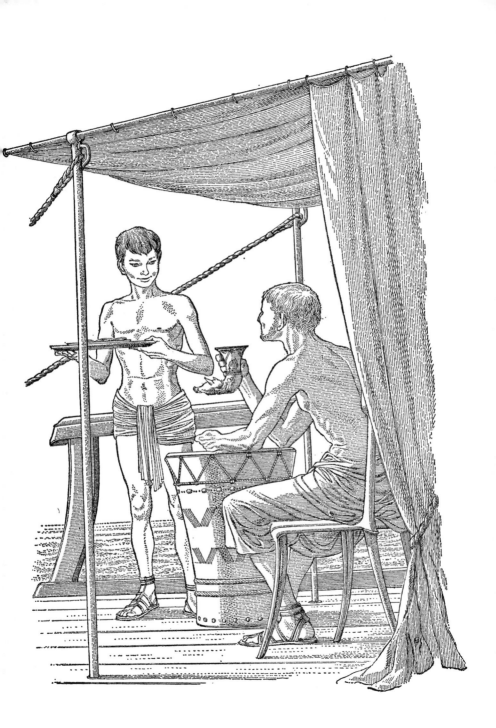

felt a surge of the old poetic joy, glimpsing bright Apollo among the dancing Muses. Then the vision was gone and he was left with his sorrow, remembering the smoking ruin that had been his city and the unburied shades of his family.

On the next day, as they stood in for the Piraeus, they were met by a Roman trireme. Dion, half asleep behind the cloak, was roused by Sabinus's sudden entrance.

"Quick!" he whispered. "Here! The curtain is double in this one place. Crawl in, lie on your side, and do not move a finger. The Romans are boarding us."

Throwing his cloak about his shoulders, as if he had gone into the tent to fetch it, Sabinus strode out on deck to welcome the officer from the trireme who was coming aboard, followed by two or three legionnaires. After the first greetings the Roman said, "At the time you sailed from Corinth, a Greek boy disappeared. His name is Dion, son of Hermonax, and he is descended from Timoleon, who was once famous in Corinth. Lucius Mummius wishes his return and we are here to ask if you have seen him and, if he is with you, to take him back with us."

"No such boy is with me," said Sabinus. "The only boy on the *Sea-Swallow* is the ship's boy, Nico. Come here, Nico. You can see he is no Corinthian."

"You say you have never seen this Dion?"

Sabinus avoided the trap.

"Was he the boy to whom Lucius Mummius gave safe conduct? There was such a boy, I think. Mummius told him to get off into the country and for all I know that's what he did. Have they searched the farms and sheepfolds?"

"Searched them!" said the officer. "Yes, they have searched

them. And now we are casting a wider net. Call your crew together. I have a word to say to them."

To the listening Dion it was an ominous word. It offered a large reward to anyone who would tell where he, Dion, might be found. And it threatened a quick death to anyone who might knowingly conceal him.

The crew listened in silence. Then there was a restless moving of feet and, one by one, beginning with Simmios the boatswain, the sailors denied all knowledge of such a stowaway. Nico was the last to speak and when he, too, denied it, there was still that hint of laughter in his voice, which always puzzled and disturbed Dion.

"Search!" ordered the officer, "and it will be the worse for you, Captain, if the boy is found."

"While the men search, may I offer you some particularly good Chion wine?" Sabinus asked in the same undisturbed voice. "You can watch from a chair by my tent. The vessel is small. It will not take your men long."

But the officer would not sit or drink. Dion could hear him pacing the deck, overseeing the men as, with upheld torches, they rummaged through the dark hold, looked behind the few remaining amphorae of wine, pushed the bundles of merchandise about, or poked in dark corners with their spears. Then they went through the crew's quarters in much the same way, lifting the mats and shaking the cloaks, but still finding nothing.

Only the captain's tent remained. Sabinus flung back the curtain which served as doorway, letting in the sunlight to the furthest corner. "Please handle my little chest carefully," he said. "I have some cups in there that I value."

How daring he is, thought Dion, never moving a muscle. Those cups he brought from Corinth. If these barbarians guessed their value, they would ask questions which Sabinus might find hard to answer.

With the cloak gone, the tent lay open and luminous. There was the captain's mattress which a soldier lifted without expectation; the little chest, not large enough to hide a three-year-old child, which another soldier nevertheless opened and looked behind; the rolled sheepskin which they opened and shook out. There was the light chair which could hide nothing. It stood in front of the double fold of canvas in which Dion lay, and when a soldier picked it up and put it down again, his sandaled feet were within inches of the boy's body.

If I should sneeze, thought Dion, but he did not sneeze or move a muscle, and at last, with a further terse threat and a repeated promise of a reward to any informer, the officer and his men were rowed back to the trireme. Life on board the *Sea-Swallow* returned to its usual routine. For an hour or more Dion lay motionless in the pocket of canvas that had served him so well, and not until the crew was eating on the foredeck did Sabinus hang up his cloak and touch Dion on the shoulder as a signal that he might now return to his usual position, while he himself sat down in his chair on the deck and called loudly to Nico to bring him bread, cheese, olives, and wine, and to be quick about it.

At the Piraeus they traded; at Cape Sunnium, off the temple of Poseidon, they lay to and offered a young goat and a whole amphora of wine to the god of the sea in thanks for a prosperous voyage. But Poseidon must have been drowsing, for the next day a storm blew up, thunder roared, lightning split the clouds, the winds whined and screamed in the bare rigging, and the sea lashed back at the winds' attack. Now the vessel shuddered and struggled to keep afloat. The straining frame cried out, the swallow figurehead plunged again and again under the sea, the black waves washed over the deck. Wind-driven spray pelted against the frail tent in which Dion stood clinging to the threshing upright, with water tugging at his feet, and water running down all his body from the spray-soaked canvas above.

Soon I shall be with the others, Dion thought. Father, I have done what I could to obey you, but some god wills otherwise.

Standing there, looking thin and bedraggled, his fair hair straggling across his face, his young mouth set, his head held up, the boy still had that air of being descended from great men—a look of character, which had drawn Lucius Mummius's attention to him outside the walls of Corinth and later had made Sabinus take heavy risks for his sake. Dion was not afraid and he was not sorry to die. His would be a good death and under the waves he would forget Corinth and the end of all whom he had loved in Corinth.

But perhaps Poseidon woke and remembered the young goat, its horns wreathed with a garland of marigolds, and the good wine. Catching up his trident, he ordered forth his chariot of shell and his plunging sea horses, and surrounded by the Nereids sped into the storm; and at his coming the winds shrank away, the clouds parted their curtains to show a sky tender and blue, the lightning withered, and the angry waves submitted to their master.

Now Dion could again hear the voices of officers and sailors. Several men were offering prayers to Poseidon or to Apollo at the small ship's altar, others were bringing a new steering oar to take the place of the starboard one that had splintered, and still others were busy recoiling ropes and spreading the wet sails to dry.

Then came the cheerful shout of Sabinus.

"Boy! boy! Where is my chair? There it is, lashed to the top of the cabin. Bring it down and spread a fresh cloth. I am hungry as a tunny-fish."

Chapter 3

The long ordeal of remaining hidden in such small space was almost over for Dion. The *Sea-Swallow* was moored to the wharf at Delos, the crowd which had come to meet it was gone and with it the crew, each man returning to his own house and household. Even Sabinus was gone. "But I will return for you and my cloak before cockcrow," he had whispered. "Only old Nicias is aboard as watchman. He always falls asleep. You will hear him snoring. But be careful still. Soon you will be safe."

When Dion heard the thin, whistling snore of the old man, he raised the curtain of the tent a little way so that he might see Delos in the light of a waning moon. This was the holy island sacred to the birth of Apollo, the sun god, and of his sister Artemis, the huntress and cold white goddess of the moon. But it was not of Artemis, only of Apollo that Dion thought, of Apollo of the glorious outpouring light, of Apollo of the Lyre who led the dance of the Muses and was the patron of dance and song and of poetry. He looked eagerly toward the low mountain of Cynthus, with its cave sacred to the dark oracle of the god. Below it he could make out the crouched stone guardian lionesses and the palm tree, under which Apollo and Artemis were said to have been born, and, nearer at hand, stood the great temple itself and the houses of the merchants and people of the place. Dion watched in awe. This small rocky island was Delos, the holiest place in all Greece, holier even than holy Delphi. "Divine Apollo, look upon me in pity," Dion prayed, but he did not feel that the god heard him. Apollo had no pity. He had joy, which welled out of him, bright and fierce, but for sorrow and despair he had no more feeling than did his sister, the moon.

Whatever happens, I have seen Delos, Dion thought, and in his deep absorption he did not hear light footsteps crossing the deck and he jerked with surprise when a hand touched his shoulder.

"Hush," whispered the voice of Nico. "And quick! Take the cloak to hide your white tunic. Old Nicias is still asleep. Over the side with you and follow me. I'll explain later."

"But Sabinus told me to stay here."

"You'll be caught like a mouse in a trap if you do. Sabinus does not know what I know. Come!"

Should he go or stay? His instinct told him to trust Nico. The ship's boy must have known all along that he was on board and had not betrayed him. A boy could judge a boy.

Dion caught down Sabinus's cloak hanging as usual at the back of the tent, and followed Nico to the deck and down the side of the *Sea-Swallow*, urged all the time by the pull of his companion's hand. They scurried off the wharf and across the beach and flung themselves into the shadow of a fishing boat pulled up on the sand. For a little while they could hear nothing but their own panting.

"Why?" Dion began, but Nico's brown hand slid over his mouth.

And now Dion could hear the sound of sandals moving softly down the roadway and along the wharf. From where they lay, twin darknesses in a deeper darkness, they saw two figures moving toward the vessel. They paused, and one said, very low, "I do not want the reward, but if Sabinus—goes, shall we say, to Rome to answer charges against him—I want the *Sea-Swallow*. Is that understood?"

"There should be no difficulty about that."

"You swear by Zeus?"

"I swear by Zeus, if the boy is there and is the one Lucius Mummius wants."

"I have no doubt of that. When I went to see to the unloading of the captain's chest I happened to brush against the cloak hanging in a corner of the tent. I felt something solid. Then I listened very carefully and I could hear the sound of light breathing. He's there. I swear to it."

"Let us go then. What about the watchman?"

"Nothing can keep old Nicias awake. That Sabinus chose him as watchman proves that he means to take off the boy tonight."

"We may be too late, then."

"No, I've had a watch kept on his house. He has not left it yet."

"Come, then."

As the men moved to the side of the *Sea-Swallow*, Dion whispered, "But that was the boatswain, Simmios. I know his voice."

"Yes, that was Simmios who has sailed with Sabinus for ten years and is his shadow. But even shadows want things and he wants the master's vessel. I am going now. Stay here. A girl will come. She is the youngest of Sabinus's seven daughters and her name is Ione. Do whatever she tells you. She serves a god and no one asks where or why she goes and comes, or what she does." And before Dion could speak, Nico was gone, slipping from shadow to shadow, and almost immediately disappearing from sight.

It was some time before the men reappeared. They must have searched the whole vessel and even old Nicias had been awakened, for Dion heard his voice and that of the boatswain giving sharp orders. As they passed Dion's hiding place, Simmios and the Roman agent were quarreling. "But I tell you," Simmios was protesting, and the other mimicked, "And *I* tell *you* not to bring me out in the middle of the night on such fools' errands. Next time you dream, you idiot, turn over in bed and go to sleep again."

When they were gone, Dion lay thinking. This is Delos. I lie here in the shadow of the god. And as so often, his thoughts turned to poetry and he repeated to himself the words of the ancient Homeric hymn to Delian Apollo in which the island itself speaks humbly, aware that the god is to be born on its rocky shores:

"How shall I receive the god, the proud
    one,
The arrogant one who stands in the
    highest place
Above all the gods and people of the
    teeming earth?
My heart is fearful at the thought of his
    coming,
For when he sees me at the first leap
    of the sunrise
Surely he will despise me, a heap of barren stones!
He will press his foot on me, he will thrust me
Into the depths of the sea, and the waves
    will wash over me,
And then he will turn away into another place
And build his temples in a land of fruitful trees,
And I shall be lost in the dark sea. Only the
    black seals
And the octopuses shall live on me. . . ."

Dion was still absorbed in the beauty of the poem when some sound roused him and he looked up to see a girl standing beside him. She was very young, and her hair was drawn back from her face and held at the nape of her neck by a pierced sea shell, through which it flowed, like pale falling water, down her back.

"Dion," she said in a light, clear voice, "I am Ione. Come."

As he rose from his hiding place to follow her, a dark cloud passed across the moon and all the beach lay in the safety of deep shadow. The girl was carrying a heavy basket and Dion helped her lift it into the bow of a skiff, which lay just above the reach of the tide. Together they pushed the boat into the water and she took the oars, motioning him to sit in the stern. The cloud shadow held on the harbor but allowed the moonlight to fall on the white rocky islands and islets which circled Delos like a ring of dancers, the Wheeling Cyclades—Syros, Tenos, Mykonos, Naxos, and Paros—he knew some of their names, but not which was which. Their cliffs shone like the robes of girls at a festival. As the boat moved, they seemed to change places between the moon and the sea, while Ione bent and straightened, bent and straightened at the pale oars.

"Ione?" Dion said at last. "Was not Ione one of the Nereids?"

"She was the youngest of them, as I am the youngest of my father's daughters," the girl answered.

After that they were both silent. Presently Dion saw that they were approaching an islet with high white cliffs, from which at some time whole slides of rock had been broken, now ringing the place in a circle of reefs and stony fangs. Ione rowed straight for a narrow passage between two such rocks and, shipping her oars, let the skiff slide forward where only a small boat could have gone. On the other side, they found themselves in calm water, heaving a little with the swells of the outer channel. Here they were in bright moonlight and Dion could see far into the depths below him, where fish swam above their shadows, dark on milk-white sand.

Abruptly the skiff swung again toward the cliff and they entered a cave, whose uneven roof was laced with moving reflections of moonlight on ripples. Things rustled overhead and other things, with sleek heads like the heads of drowned men, slid into the water from a shelf of sand at the far end of the cavern and swam past them.

"Bats," explained Ione. "And seals."

A moment later the skiff grounded on a beach only large enough for so small a boat, and Ione stepped out, taking the basket.

"No," she said to Dion's offer of help. "I am used to it. The path is rough. Go ahead so that you may find your way in the moonlight."

Only later did he guess that the girl had lingered behind so that he might be alone in the valley to which he climbed. It was a small place, a dark hollow between the cliffs, but it looked larger in the moonlight. The shrine which stood there was small and ruinous, but its thick pillars and starkness made it too seem larger than it was. Some of the roof had fallen in and moonlight lay on the altar which was empty of all but a fishing spear and one moon-bright fish. Dark weeds grew between the stones of the steps, and dark vines trailed from the broken roof. The inscription across the lintel was not easy to read through the rosettes of lichen which dappled the stone, but Dion at last made it out: "To Loneliness."

To Loneliness! Was Loneliness also a god? There had been no temple to him in rich and busy Corinth. But this was the god for whom his soul in its despair had cried out. For a minute he stood before the shrine in prayer and then wrapped himself in Sabinus's borrowed cloak and went to sleep, his head pillowed upon the lowest of the crumbling steps.

Chapter 4

The rising sun woke Dion. He sat up and looked about him. Not a living creature moved in the hollow valley between the cliffs, but the air was filled with the cries and the mazy dancing of the gulls, sharing the dance of light, which made even the white cliffs vibrate and pulse in their eternal places. All things seemed to move, to leap, to become part of the light which shone down upon them, and beyond the reefs Dion could hear the ring of waves, dancing too, and shining too, he knew, though he could not see them. The shrine behind him was so hidden in its valley that only the birds could know that it was there. In the sunlight it seemed smaller, but it had lost none of its air of remoteness. Solid and indifferent, it withheld itself from the joy of the sun. Its pillars and walls were stained with age and the shadows it cast were massive and unyielding. If stone can brood, the shrine brooded and Dion turned from the bright challenge of Apollo to the presence of this remote and indifferent god.

As he stood before the altar to pray, he saw that the offering had been changed and that now a few flowers and a small basket of brown eggs stood where the fish and spear had lain. Someone had been here already, but he had heard no step or rustle of garments. Whoever served this altar, served it in silence.

For a long time Dion remained in the temple, absorbed in its mindless calm. Hunger and a faint stirring of curiosity at last drove him out to explore. There were more sounds now, a chirring of grasshoppers and a humming of bees among the thyme and once a barking which he took to be the barking of a seal beyond the cliffs. A path led him a little uphill toward a gate between rock ledges. On the other side he found a second valley no larger than the first and, like it, hidden from the sea. But in this valley there was life. Beside the sparkle of a spring, a cottage of stone and thatch stood against the cliffs, its roof overspread by a great fig tree. To one side, grape vines grew over an arbor with two olive trees beyond, as ancient as the fig. Hens and a rooster pecked about in the shade and three goats cropped the short herbage, while a kid played a lonely game with its shadow.

Where are the people? Dion thought. And as if in answer, an old woman appeared in the doorway of the house. Dion had never seen a woman so tall, so old, or with such a look of strength. She was dressed in a robe of blue so dark that it appeared to be almost black, and her long gray hair showed like a mane under a veil of the same blue-black color.

"Welcome, Dion," she said in a voice which had no hint of age in it. "I am Erinna, the priestess of this temple. You are hungry and here is food."

She served him in silence, which he found a little difficult to break, but at last he said, "I did not know that there was a god of Loneliness."

"A great god," said Erinna. "People have forgotten how great. He works with Asclepius, the Healer. Those, too, who serve Apollo, turn to him. But like all gods, he can be cruel. Pan has met him often in the high solitudes, where men go mad."

She said no more, but left him to eat his meal of coarse bread, goat's milk, cheese, and black olives, while she worked in the garden on the other side of the house. The peace in this valley was almost as deep as that in the valley of the shrine. When Dion had eaten, he went to find the old woman.

"May I help you, Erinna?" he asked.

"No," she said. "For today explore this little country. Only never stand against the sky. It is the god's will that we live unknown."

He waited a moment in case she had something more to say, but she seemed to have forgotten him, and he wandered off. The cliffs were delightful to explore, filled with secret places carpeted with flowers, luring him to lie, half asleep, watching the clouds—for a little while free from his burden of thought. He had glimpses, too, of the sea, but he remembered Erinna's warning and was careful to take no chances of being seen from some passing fishing boat. In time he found a buttress of rock behind which he could climb down to the level of the tides.

When the sun's chariot blazed from highest heaven he came upon Ione at the edge of a narrow gulf. She had been fishing, but now sat motionless, looking down at the water whose pulse swayed back and forth, moving the long green seaweed, fine as a Nereid's hair. She looked up and smiled at him briefly, then returned to her contemplation. Dion was beginning to know the ways of those who served the god. He found a seat of rock almost out of sight of Ione, and he, too, watched the ebb and flow of the water until he was hypnotized by it.

The land crumbles and cities fall to ruin, he thought, but the sea never changes and the Nereids are forever young, and it comforted him to know that far away the waves of the gulf broke on the desolate shores of Corinth, but were themselves untouched by all the fury of Rome.

Was it for this reason that his thoughts were now occupied with Nereids? Or was it because of Ione? He leaned forward to look at her. Her head was turned away. He saw her cheek, smooth as a wave-worn stone, and her hair rippling from the pierced shell which held it. Could it be possible that she was truly a sea nymph, and no daughter at all to the merchant who had befriended him? Here on the island of the god such a presence would not be strange. And Erinna—she did not seem like a woman, but like Demeter, the goddess of earth and its richness. Did the Immortals walk this hidden isle?

For a long time he sat, lost in wonder, but surely, he told himself, he was not worthy to live among the gods. This girl, this tall old woman, must be what they said they were, human like himself. Yet the doubt remained and cast a strangeness over all his thoughts.

Chapter 5

The first day set the pattern for the others. Each person went his or her own way and very little was said when they met at the morning and evening meal. At Dion's request, Erinna taught him how to milk the two nanny goats. He had never done any work with his hands, having spent his time in the study of philosophy and history and oratory or under the stern discipline of the gymnasium, where he had run and wrestled, thrown the discus and the javelin, and practiced swordplay with the other boys. He was neither the best (as his father could have wished) nor the worst in his group, and was always grudging the time that might have been spent in learning the long, great art of poetry.

On the third morning Ione left for Delos.

"She will be back," said Erinna.

"Are you not afraid that she may be followed, Erinna?" Dion asked.

"No, everyone understands that she serves a god. Not long after he had called her here, a fisherman tried to follow her to find out where she went. A wind came up. Ione reached the cave in safety, but his boat was wrecked on the rocks and his body has never been found. No one has followed her since."

The old woman picked up her distaff and was about to relapse into her calm silence. But Dion asked her another question.

"She is not one of the Immortals?"

Erinna shook her head, with no sign of surprise.

"No, she is Sabinus's youngest daughter, as you have been told. The god called her from a household noisy with the talk of a mother and six chattering sisters."

"Sabinus permits her to come and go?"

"She is nearer to his heart than all the rest, and he knows that she serves a god."

Dion would have liked to ask more, but Erinna again picked up her distaff and stood looking out toward the evening sky where the first stars were beginning to appear, and Dion went back to the shrine for his evening prayer and his quiet sleep at the steps. His dreams were no longer haunted by his father's presence, red with wounds. He no longer reached out in nightmare to stop his mother before she took the fatal step from the well-curb, or tried in vain to catch at the wrists of the Roman soldiers as they cut down his tutor with their short swords. If he dreamed of his family at all, it was as they used to be, smiling a welcome as he returned with his tutor from gymnasium or forum.

One afternoon Dion climbed to the top of a solitary rock which rose from the hollow of ground near the shrine. The sun warmed his head and shoulders like a hand laid upon them, and the hum of bees in the wild thyme, joined to the metallic whir of the cicadas, was so loud, and the hot, clear air seemed so bright and pulsing about him, that at last the boy grew drowsy. Between sleeping and waking his thoughts returned to a day more than a year before when he had climbed to the citadel at Corinth. It was the first time he had been there alone, and he saw everything with undulled eyes, beautiful and fresh and holy. Apollo had seemed then to be an almost visible presence beside him, and now again he felt the presence of the god, as in memory he climbed the steep road to the high rocky helmet of the Acrocorinth which crowned the city. Once again in his mind Dion paused to speak to the guards at the gate and then walked up the stony way past holy springs and small temples. He remembered the gray shrine to Necessity and Force—not much larger than this shrine to Loneliness. Looking down, he could see in his imagination the rich city of Corinth below him, with its squares and colonnades, and beyond Corinth the silken blue of the Saronic Gulf and the Gulf of Corinth, separated by the narrow isthmus across which vessels, smaller than grape seeds, were moving from one gulf to the other, slowly dragged on rollers by long lines of men and animals. Then the isthmus widened into the stretches of green land where stood the temple of Poseidon, where once every two years the Isthmaic games had been held, and beyond these lowlands rose the circle of mountains, like folds in the robes of great reclining goddesses of stone.

This was the first time Dion's thoughts had returned to Corinth for more than a moment. Until now his grief had always risen to drive his memories back. But something had changed. He could remember and feel no pain, only the old familiar pleasure. Once more he stood on the terrace before the highest shrine, the temple of the armed Aphrodite, and looked over land and sea toward the distant witnessing mountains.

Great Corinth is fallen, he thought. The city is now only rubble and broken columns. The shrines are robbed, the statues of our gods stand on Roman altars. But the sea, the blue twin gulfs, are as they were before the Romans came.

The Nereids! And suddenly his thoughts caught fire. Although he was the only human being in the hollow meadow he felt great presences about him—Loneliness with shadowed face and bright Apollo.

Quickly he dropped from the rock and stood with his feet planted on the earth and his arms outstretched, palms upward. And it seemed to him that the words he chanted were both his and not his.

> "Where is thine admired beauty,
>   Dorian Corinth?
> Where is thy crown of towers? Where are thy
>   treasures of old?
> Where now are the temples of the gods?
>   And thy crowded theaters and forums?
> Not even a trace, O saddest

of all sad cities, is left of thee,
And war has devoured thee
and all that was thine.
Only we, the ageless sea nymphs,
maidens of ocean, abide,
Halcyons wailing for thy woes."

He had been standing in the ecstasy of poetic creation, but as he finished his chant, already the vision of what he had meant to say was fading, leaving only his actual words, dull as beach pebbles when the tide goes out. Yet Dion was not discouraged. The great thing was that he had made a beginning. He knew himself as only half-trained, and a boy. With Apollo's aid, he would yet seek out masters and learn the necessary skill. Someday he would make such poems to the beauty and woes of Corinth that all Greece should remember her and mourn again for her loss.

As the glory slowly departed, Dion found new emotions stirring in him, like spring flowers rising through the dead covering of autumn leaves. Strong and alive rose his gratitude toward Sabinus who had risked so much for him, and with it came his liking for that other boy, Nico, who had not betrayed him. Besides these, he felt a deep reverence for Erinna, but for Ione there was some even stronger feeling which he could not understand, since he had never felt it before. All these emotions had stirred in him earlier, but faintly, as if another person were experiencing them. Now, at last, the great act of creation had made him whole, knowing joy as well as sorrow, and a kinship to the living as well as to the dead.

Chapter 6

That evening at supper Erinna as usual sat in silence, but after the meal she turned to Dion.

"What has happened, Dion? The gods have spoken to you?"

"Yes," he said. "Both the god of this island and Apollo, I think. They gave me words for my grief and now I can face it."

"Grief is a strength," the old woman said, "when it has been met and looked in the eyes. It may be that it is now time for you to go. If so, the gods will tell us how and by what means. Ione should be back tomorrow. She will bring the news of Delos."

It was nearly noon before Ione appeared, carrying her basket filled with new-baked bread, a bunch of watercress, and a few roses for the altar, her feet as always moving almost in silence and her face as calm as her limpid voice. She brought messages from her father, Sabinus. Simmios and the Roman agent were watching every one who came in and out of Sabinus's house, and Simmios, on one pretext or another, had forced his way into the hearth at unexpected hours. Delos was still unsafe for Dion and would be until after Lucius Mummius and the army had returned to Rome and been awarded their triumph.

"Did you see Nico?" Dion asked, eagerly.

Ione gave him a quick glance and a little nod.

"I passed him among the houses. He lifted his brows. I smiled. He knows that you are safe."

That day Erinna ate nothing and in the late afternoon she went into the cottage and came out dressed in white, with a white veil almost covering her face. In silence she motioned the other two to follow, and in silence they obeyed. When they came to the shrine, Erinna went in, leaving them at the threshold, and, after praying before the altar, parted the heavy curtains behind it and disappeared from sight.

"She has entered the holy of holies," whispered Ione as she moved nearer to Dion. Her voice trembled. "Once I looked into it. It is a cave filled with a rushing sound."

Dion reached out for her hand, but he was in too great awe to speak. Later, he could not have said whether the time was long or short before the curtains parted again and Erinna came out, pale, upright, foam on her lips and her gaze fixed straight before her. Like a sleepwalker she returned to the house and went in, closing the door behind her.

Some time later she came out in her usual blue-black robes and veil, and sat down wearily by the spring, trailing one hand in the cold water.

When at last she looked up, she seemed surprised to find the others there.

"It is as I thought," she said in an exhausted voice. "The god's work is finished. Dion is to leave the island, but when and how I was not told."

Dion looked at Ione, and saw in her eyes a suddenly stricken look, but she did not speak.

"What of Ione?" he asked.

"Ione?" repeated Erinna. "Ione? Ione serves the god while I live. But when I die, she is free. This god requires neither priests nor worshipers, or if he wishes them, he will summon them. When the time comes, you may have Ione if her father is willing. And if she wishes it, it will be his wish."

Under the demand in Dion's gray eyes, Ione's face flushed red and then turned white again.

"When the time comes I will be ready, Dion," she said steadily, but so low that he could scarcely hear her voice, and soon she went into the house, closing the door softly.

Chapter 7

The three returned to their usual life on the island, living almost in silence. Dion continued to sleep on the steps of the shrine in fair weather, and on the floor before the altar when it rained. He helped the others at the chores, digging in the garden, milking the goats, fishing in the clefts of the cliffs, and as he worked with his hands, words and phrases came into his mind, sparkling with poetry, like bits of quartz crystal suddenly bright in the arrowed light of Apollo. His thoughts, long dulled by grief, now came alive again, and with their life there followed a new restlessness. It was time for him to leave the island, and he found it hard to wait on the will of the god, not knowing whether he might be dismissed in hours, days, months, or even years. Ione perhaps felt something of the same uncertainty. She often daydreamed, a dif-

ferent quiet from her old tranquility. Now her eyes followed
Dion wherever he went.

Only Erinna went about her daily life unaffected by the
imminence of coming change. Tall, slow, in her dark rai-
ment, she moved, as brooding as some statue in the shrine to
Loneliness to which breath had been given by the godhead.
But even Erinna seemed, perhaps, to look more often than
usual at sky and clouds, to listen more intently to the sounds
of the winds and waves that ringed the island.

Yet when the dawn of the day for which all three waited
arrived at last, it gave no warning to the watchers. The sun
rose triumphant, like a dancer taking the first steps of a
dance, and the waves clapped their hands lightly in rhythm.
No sound came from the shadowed shrine, no snake moved
at Dion's feet to tell him that this was a day not as other days,
and Erinna's offering lay undisturbed on the dark altar.

At midmorning three triremes beat in for Delos, making
slow headway in the hot faint wind. Dion watched them idly
and did not know that the other two were beside him until
Erinna spoke.

"They are from Athens," she said. "See the figureheads of
the helmeted Athena at their prows. They are perhaps bringing offerings to the Delian Apollo."

The northern channel between the islands was narrow and
used only in calm weather, but the sluggish Athenian vessels
chose it as the nearest. The first two passed slowly into the
sheltered water which surrounded Delos, but as the last and
smallest trireme came abreast the cliffs, a thirty-foot wave rose
out of the quiet sea and rushed upon the ship in a charging
wall of arching water and torn foam. The steersmen tried to

turn the prow to meet the attack, but the vessel had too little headway to move quickly, and a moment later the downpouring wave struck the ship, crashing the hull against the rocks and tearing every person from its decks.

The whole thing happened in the wink of an eye, like some nightmare dreamed between blue sky and blue sea. Dion gasped and turned pale and then began to climb quickly down the side of the nearest cliff, careless of his own safety.

Halfway down, his hands and legs scraped and bleeding, he was aware that Ione was close behind him.

"Go back!" he shouted, but she neither answered nor obeyed.

At the foot of the cliff there was the usual jumble of great rocks, most of them jagged and all bearded with green seaweed and rough with barnacles. Jammed between two of these lay the gaping and empty vessel, its prow raised high against the radiant sky as if protesting the doom which had come so suddenly upon it. Dion went as near as he could to the wreck, shouting, but no one answered. Once he thought that he saw, far-off, the bodies of two men, but if he had seen them at all, they were a moment later sucked under the sliding surface of the sea.

"Here he is," called Erinna, bending over something wedged behind a boulder. How and when the old priestess had reached the scene, Dion did not then guess. But she was there and the man she had so confidently expected to find was there also, and alive, though at the moment barely conscious.

Dion and Ione hurried to the place, slipping and sliding on the wet green shingle, and arriving breathless to find Erinna feeling the castaway for broken bones.

She looked up.

"He is only bruised and bewildered," she said. "Let him come to himself. No harm can touch him."

By her words they knew that the priestess believed the man to have been brought by some god, and they were in no doubt that it was the god of the island working through Poseidon. Only for Poseidon were the waves of the sea bound or set loose. In Corinth Dion had once heard a philosopher say that at long intervals of time these solitary great waves rose from the deep after an earthquake had shaken the bottom of the ocean. Perhaps so. But who had roused the earthquake? Who but Poseidon, answering some appeal of the god of their broken shrine?

As he waited, Dion studied the stranger. He was a man of middle age with a heavy body and a face bearded and authoritative, despite its cuts and bruises. He was not dressed like a seaman, and his garments, though torn and dragging with the wetness of the sea, were those of a man of wealth. He must have been looking under lowered lids at Dion and the women for some time before he startled them by speaking.

"Where is the vessel?" he asked.

Dion pointed. "Wrecked," he said.

"And the men?"

"You are the only one to reach the shore."

"And this shore?"

Erinna answered before Dion could speak.

"It is an island not far from Delos and sacred to a god. A message will be sent to the other ships telling them of your safety, and a little later it will be arranged for you to join them. My name is Erinna and I am priestess of this place. The boy is Dion, son of Hermonax of Corinth, and the girl Ione, daughter of Sabinus the Roman, Delian born."

The stranger had followed Erinna's words carefully, glancing at Dion and Ione as their names were mentioned. To Dion, who had looked startled at finding his city so openly named, he said, with the slightest of smiles, "You have nothing to fear from me, Dion, son of Hermonax. I am an Athenian and no friend to Rome. My name is Agios, son of Proxenos, and I am on a mission from Athens to Alexandria."

The return to the house was not as difficult as Dion had foreseen. Erinna led the way to a path, almost a rough staircase, behind one of the abutments of the cliff, its entrance at each end so cleverly hidden by boulders that not even Ione had known of its existence. Up this Dion and Ione helped Agios, a few steps at a time, and as he climbed he seemed to gain in strength, so that he walked unaided across the goats' grazing meadow to Erinna's house, where he went to sleep on the couch under a goatskin rug, after drinking an herb brew which the priestess brought him in a painted cup.

Some hours later, Agios rejoined them, almost completely recovered from the terrors of the shipwreck. While he slept, Erinna and Ione had washed, dried, and mended his garments, and now Agios thanked all three for the care they had taken of him.

"If you had not come, I should have died at the sea's edge like my unfortunate companions," he said. "How may I repay you? Is there any gift that I may make to the god you serve?"

Erinna shook her head.

"There is no gift," she said. "But still there is a return that you may make, if you wish. How long will the triremes stay at Delos?"

"They will take the offerings from Athens to Apollo's shrine. Sostratos, the captain of the larger vessel, will certainly act in my place. I think he will then consult the oracle of Apollo on Mount Cynthus as to my fate, and after that, send the ship's boat to look for me. Food and water must be taken aboard the triremes. They will not leave for two days, at the earliest. Is it permitted me to signal to the boat when it comes?"

Erinna shook her head again.

"Even on Delos no one knows that this island is inhabited. Sabinus, himself, father of Ione, does not know where she goes when she leaves his roof. Your men are almost sure to find the wreck, but they will think that you perished with the others. There seems to be no way up the cliff, and they will be told by the Delians that the island is never visited. Tomorrow Ione will take word of your safety to Sostratos and instruct him as to what he is to do. It will be best if you yourself write to him. Dion can act as secretary, if you wish."

Agios nodded, his keen glance going from Erinna to Dion.

"So the Corinthian could replace my secretary?" he asked. "My poor Anytos died with the rest. I shall need a secretary on board ship and in Alexandria, a city not under Rome's shadow. Fortunately my credentials and papers are on the greatest of the triremes, along with my own possessions. Anytos and I transferred to the smallest of the three ships, as I always like to know the quality of the men and materials used on an expedition. These were good men. I shall erect a memorial to them when and where I can. That is all that is left for me to do for their spirits."

"I imagine," said Erinna, "that most of their bodies will be found and buried, either by their comrades or by the Delians, who know the currents hereabouts."

"They will lie more quietly in the earth, if that be the will of the gods," replied Agios gravely. "Who can say what the divine ones permit or do not permit?"

All afternoon Erinna and Agios sat talking, while Dion and Ione, who looked as if she had been crying, listened in sad silence, sitting close together, their shoulders touching, comforting one another voicelessly for the deaths of all those men who had died so suddenly before their eyes. Meanwhile the older people made their plans. In the end Agios agreed to Erinna's conditions, and it was he who suggested how Dion's Corinthian speech might be disguised until they were safe in Alexandria, beyond reach of chance or of mischance.

That night Dion did not sleep on the porch of the shrine as was his custom. The death of the Athenians still weighed upon his heart, and now the shrine seemed menacing. He remembered how Erinna, on that first day, had said that the god of Loneliness appeared in many forms. All the gods, even Phoebus Apollo, had their dark aspects in which they dealt death as easily as they gave life at other times. But Dion was human and felt human pity, and that night he sought the shelter of a rock among the thyme, watching the Milky Way overhead, and, only after a long time fell asleep, and in sleep found some measure of acceptance of the mysterious wills of the gods.

Chapter 8

Next morning Ione slipped away to Delos, bearing the message from Agios to the captain. And at dawn on the second day, Agios, blindfolded, and Dion with a woolen bandage wrapped about his throat, made their way with the women across the island and down the steep slope into the cavern, where all but Erinna climbed into Ione's little boat amid the barking of seals.

Dion gave a silent blessing to the seals: "If you be drowned Athenians, may you have joy among the waters." But then he remembered that there had been just as many seals in the cave before the disaster. These might, indeed, be the spirits of drowned men as people said, but if they were, they had been lost in earlier, unknown shipwrecks.

Before Ione pushed off, Agios and Dion made their grateful farewells to Erinna. For a moment she laid her hands on Dion's hair. "Do not try to judge the gods, Dion. Their ways are not our ways." And now he could look back into her great calm eyes and say, "I do not judge, and I will all my life be grateful to you and to him whom you serve."

After leaving the cavern, Ione rowed for a while along a watery lane between cliffs and rocks. When, some distance from the cavern's mouth, she quietly steered the skiff into the roadstead, there were the two Athenian triremes waiting, their sails lowered. "You may look about you now, Agios," she told the man. "Your ships are here."

In a few minutes they were at the side of the larger trireme, eagerly greeted by the Athenians. Agios was first to go aboard, while Dion lingered for a moment handing Ione the cloak he had been wearing.

"Farewell, Ione," he said. "Take this to your father and once again give him my thanks for the life he saved. And remember, if I live I shall return for you."

"Farewell, Dion," she said. And then in a sudden rush, "Oh, be careful of yourself! Very careful! If I live, I shall be here when you come."

Still Dion lingered.

"Ione," he repeated. "Ione . . ." But Agios was calling him.

So at last, unwillingly, Dion went aboard, and when he looked back at Ione from the deck, he saw her eyes bright with so many tears that she could scarcely see to return his gesture of farewell. But at last she picked up the oars and rowed away, the skiff for once zig-zagging blindly across the water.

On the trireme there was great joy over Agios's return from the dead, and many questions to ask and to answer about the loss of the ship.

"Surely the work of some god," said Sostratos, the captain, a small intense man with gray hair and a habit of standing with his hands at his sides, half hidden among his robes. "We felt the wave, but it's force was broken by the outer islets. It lifted up the vessels and set them down again as if a hill of water had passed beneath us. And that was all. But when your trireme did not appear, we feared that some mischance had befallen her and sent out the ship's boats. They found the wreck and the scattered bodies of most of the crew and of Anytos. They now lie in the holy earth of Delos not far from the shrine of Apollo. But what happened to you, sir? We had given up all hope that anyone had been saved until a young girl brought us your message."

"The girl and her friends rescued me," said Agios, "as the gods willed. One of them is my new secretary here, Lysis, a Delian by birth. But having plunged into the sea to bring me to the beach, he caught a deep disorder of the chest and throat, and cannot speak above a whisper, poor boy."

Dion felt Sostratos's sceptical eyes upon him. But the captain asked no questions. Dion-Lysis was officially accepted on board ship and played his part, coughing from time to time and speaking with difficulty in a wheezing voice which turned almost at once into that universal whisper, in which all differences between the accent of one city and another city are lost. He avoided contact with the crew, living in Agios's quarters and eating there with him, or, on pleasant days, sitting at his feet on deck, taking down from dictation letters to the

Athenian government or to his friends there and in other places. Family Agios had none, having lost his wife by illness and his only son in war.

"I am a lonely man," he once told Dion, "but I am free. No one can suffer from my decisions," and he looked out across the waves to the far-off horizon with a glance at once dreamy and decisive. For a moment it seemed as if the older man would speak further, but he checked himself, and went on with the letter he was dictating.

Chapter 9

These days aboard ship were very different from the days of cramped hiding which Dion had spent behind Sabinus's cloak on the *Sea-Swallow*. Now when Agios had no need for him, he could do as he pleased, and though he kept to himself, he enjoyed watching the busy life of those around him. The *Swallow* had been a merchant vessel trusting entirely to her sails, but these triremes were owned by Athens, and had three banks of oars on either side, the lowest bank manned by slaves and the others by free men in the service of the state. However, for the present the winds were favoring and for the most part the sails were used, except when late in the afternoon they came into some harbor, when the oars saved time and maneuvering. One evening they put in at Naxos with its silvery white cliffs glowing rose in the sunset, and another night was spent at Santorin. Always they sailed in sight of

islands, and often there were temples on the headlands, and sometimes when their ships skirted the land, they made sacrifices to the god of that place. But to whatever god they sacrificed on occasion, the three great presences always about them were Apollo, glorious by day, and Artemis, his twin sister, who ruled the night, and Poseidon, by whose favor they sailed the shifting sea.

To all appearances on those occasions when Dion was forced to speak, the crew accepted the story of his affliction and neither laughed nor commented upon his hoarseness and whisperings. Only Sostratos, the captain, sometimes listened with a grim smile or paused beside the boy as he stood by the rail and he, like Agios, seemed sometimes about to speak seriously, but, checking himself with a shrug, made some comment about the next landfall instead.

Late one afternoon as they passed eastward along the coast of Crete they saw a trireme on their lee, apparently attempting to overhaul them. Sostratos pointed out the strange craft to Agios, and then waited, one gray eyebrow a little raised.

"Roman?" asked Agios.

"So I should think," said Sostratos.

"Always these Romans."

"Always these Romans."

"Can we outrun them?"

"With this start, I think so. They are using the oars, but we have oars, too."

"Well, let us see. We have nothing to hide, but I dislike this assumption that it is their place to question and ours to answer, like children when the schoolmaster speaks."

Sostratos gave orders, the trumpet sounded, and in a moment there was a rush of sandaled feet to the rowing benches, and then the great gong began to boom out the rhythm of the strokes, steady and strong like the heavy heartbeat of the ship itself. The men were in high spirits. Being Athenians, they loved to pit their strength and skill against others, and now they settled down to the race, grinning and joking. The deck crew shifted the sails, to catch every breath of wind and, smiling, Sostratos sacrificed to Poseidon at the ship's altar. Even Dion felt the excitement, although he knew that if the Romans succeeded in overtaking them, they would be both angry and suspicious, and that he, with his swaddled throat and croaking voice, would be a natural object for both their anger and suspicion to light upon.

Fortunately, the sun was on its western course and there was enough wind so that the small clouds swam through the blue like the porpoises which played about the bows of the two triremes.

The exaltation Dion felt was shared by everyone aboard ship, even to the slaves on the lowest benches. The race was like a festival; the rowers sang Athenian songs of victory and with every heartbeat of the gong, the three-layered oars responded and the ship shot forward like a runner whose feet scarcely touch the ground. For a time, both Greek vessels seemed to be outdistancing the heavier Roman trireme, but it did not give up the chase. Slowly, slowly, like a hound pursuing deer, it drew up on its quarry. Slowly, slowly, the details of its figurehead, the decorations of its sails, the color of the blades of its oars became clearer and clearer, until at last Dion could make out the figures of the soldiers gathered on the foredeck.

As Sostratos stood frowning at the stern, watching the on-coming of the Romans, Dion touched him on the arm. The captain turned sharply.

"What?" he demanded.

"It is no use," said Dion speaking for the first time in his natural Corinthian voice. "Let them take me. The rowers will kill themselves at the oars."

"You!" said Sostratos with a snort of laughter. "Who cares about you? I am thinking of Athens, of Greece, of our dis-honored gods. They are beginning to falter. Now is the mo-ment for us to break away."

Short, slight, and gray-haired as he was, Sostratos leaped onto the walk between the rowing benches from which the gong was sounding. Something had broken through his usual restraint. He was laughing and shouting to the man at the gong to be silent. Now he raised his hands against the blue, white-garlanded sky and Dion saw with a start that both thumbs had at some time been hacked away. Perhaps Sostra-tos was no longer conscious of the mutilation he usually sought to hide. Or perhaps he displayed it now for his own purpose as he cried to the rowers:

"The Romans have over-reached themselves. They are be-ginning to falter. Now! Now! Athenians! Draw away from them, friends, draw away, if you crack your sinews! For the honor of the Maiden, row! There will be wine tonight for every man, as much as he can hold. They have beaten us Greeks on land. Show them we are still their masters on the sea!"

From the gasping mouths of the rowers came an answering shout. Again the gong began, but faster than before. The heart of the ship was beating now like the heart of a runner on the steep slope of a hill. But the Roman hound drew no nearer, and slowly, almost imperceptibly, it began to drop back. Still like a hungry dog, it hung on, and several times even spurted forward across the darkening sea, but it never again came so close to its quarry.

Dion had been watching so intently, standing beside the silent Agios, that he had been unaware of the changes of the sky and sea above and about him, until all at once he noticed that the trireme was pitching among choppy waves, and that the porpoises at the bow had become almost invisible shapes, outlined faintly by the spray which broke against their sleek sides. Surely night had come early, and, looking up, Dion saw that the sky which had recently been so blue and white was now gray and black with gathering storm clouds covering the sun.

"Apollo has deserted us!" he exclaimed, with a shiver.

But before Agios could reply, Sostratos, who had overheard, leaped with his cat's ease from the rower's walk, and stood grinning beside them.

"Not so, boy," he answered. "Apollo holds his shield over us. Soon now the Romans will lose us in the dark, and then I shall outwit them. They will expect us to steer for the shores of Asia as we are now doing, but I shall turn and head straight south for Alexandria. In the morning they may scratch their heads to find us."

"But into the open sea?" asked Agios. "I'm not sure that I approve. It is very dangerous to sail out of sight of land!"

"Dangerous! Approve!" mocked Sostratos. "And I'm not sure that I care whether or not you approve! On land you are the envoy of Athens, but here I am captain and I decide what is dangerous!"

"Well," said Agios, "we must not quarrel. If we are to drown, I have had recent practice in it. And you need not fear that I shall report you in Athens, for once I have done the city's business in Alexandria I shall stay there. I am tired of the shadow of Rome everywhere."

So this was what Agios had intended all the time and had almost spoken of! Now in the excitement of the chase, his caution had at last worn thin.

"And I shall stay with you!" cried Dion, suddenly seeing his future clear before him.

"Until it is safe to return and fetch Ione," said Agios, smiling. "Dion, you two will find Alexandria a Greek olive tree flourishing by the Nile."

"So that is what you plan?" demanded Sostratos. "It's all right for you, old man. Your fighting days are over. But this boy is a different matter. He shall repay me for the thumbs the Romans took, making me unfit for spear or bow or oar or sickle or any other instrument. But they made a bad bargain, for without my hands I have had to use my wits. Now you, Lysis-Dion or whatever your name is, shall be my hands and I shall be your brains, cunning in vengeance. North of the Black Sea live the tribes that follow their horse herds. They despise the Greeks but they hate Rome. Some day they will ride through the Roman forum with bloody spears, if it takes them five hundred years. To them the boy and I will go and do our little to speed that day. Eh, boy? Answer like a man."

Dion spoke slowly.

"I do not think such was my father's will. I think that at

the last, standing at the edge of ruin, my father was willing
for me to follow my own path. He said, 'Keep our name illus-
trious.' I think he meant in my own way, as a poet, since he
knew that I am dedicated to the service of Apollo and the
Muses. At that last hour, he did not speak of war, nor of vengeance, but only of renown.''

"Is he dead then, or a slave? And the rest of your family?
Oh, I knew from the first that you were a Corinthian noble.
It takes more than a woolen cloth about your neck to disguise
one of your breeding! Your city is in ashes, the altars pro-
faned! And you hesitate! What of your family?"

"Dead."

"And you hesitate? By Poseidon! I shall spend the rest of
my days avenging two thumbs, and you hesitate to make the
Romans answer for your dead! What runs in your veins?
Milk or blood?"

Dion turned helplessly toward Agios, but the Athenian
was looking out over the dark horizon of waves, his face sad
in the dim light. Dion alone must make the decision, and
half of him said, "You must sacrifice all you now love and
wish to be for the sake of those you once loved, and go with
this man to a life you hate." He did not think that his father's
shade required it of him. Yet it might be that this was what
was demanded by Corinth, fallen and desolate.

But before the words could be said, something happened
which drew the eyes of all three to the sky. From among the
shifting clouds the sun now all at once sent out a long ray of
golden light, falling from its unseen disk down to the tossing
sea. Then the light, brightening, seemed to move as if search-
ing for something, sweeping slowly along the waves like a

blind man's hand, touching briefly the smaller trireme and then coming to rest on the deck of the greater ship, glowing along the oars of the rowers, gilding the rigging, shining on the dolphins' wet backs, bringing a brightness to every tired upturned face. But in all this effulgence, the core and fire of the shaft rested on Dion and there it held motionless for what seemed a long time.

All shining, Dion stood between the two men who stared at him in silence. He was for that moment radiant and outlined in radiance, taller than in daily life and perfectly serene, like a young priest of Apollo. Sostratos stared and drew one thumbless hand across his eyes and turned away.

In his mood of exaltation, Dion remembered what Sabinus, Ione's father, had said on that first day under the doomed walls of Corinth: "Perhaps we follow the god who chooses us and have ourselves no choice in the matter."

"The god has chosen," he exclaimed joyfully, all his uncertainty burned away in the divine light which held him in its center. "My thanks, O Great One!" and he stretched out his hands in the ritual gesture of worship, and beside him, Agios stretched out his hands, also, in thanks to Apollo for his divine judgment. As they gave thanks to the god, the light withdrew slowly, growing fainter and fainter, and then once more the darkness of Apollo's shield was spread over them and the triremes, hidden from the eyes of the Romans, turned and sought the open sea, their prows headed for Alexandria.